HOLIDAY WISHES

USA TODAY BESTSELLING AUTHOR

S.L. STERLING

HOLIDAY WISHES

S.L. STERLING

Holiday Wishes

Copyright © 2020 by S.L. Sterling

All rights reserved. Without limiting the rights under copyright reserved about, no part of this publication may be reproduced, stored in, or introduced into a retrieval system, or transmitted in any form or by any means (mechanical, electronic, photocopying, recording, or otherwise) without the prior written permission of both the copyright owner and the above publisher of the book. This is a work of fiction. Any references to historical events, real people, or real places are used fictitiously. Other names, characters, places, and events are products of the author's imagination, and any resemblance to actual events or places or persons, living or dead, is entirely coincidental. Disclaimer: This book contains mature content not suitable for those under the age of 18. It involves strong language and sexual situations. All parties portrayed in sexual situations are consenting adults over the age of 18.

Paperback ISBN: 978-1-989566-15-2

Ebook ISBN: 978-1-989566-14-5

Editor: Brandi Aquino, Editing Done Write

Cover Design: KL Donn, Alluring Write Productions

Created with Vellum

Welcome to Santa Claus, Indiana where Christmas isn't just a holiday, it's a way of life. Join these 12 amazing authors with 11 wonderful books as they bring you some instalove, a little mystery, and maybe some thriller, for a romance filled holiday!

The community of Santa Claus was designed in 1849. The story of how it received the name of Santa Claus has roots both in fact and legend. In January 1856 the town applied for a post office to be installed.

On June 25, 1895, as part of a nationwide standardization for place names, the post office name was changed to the one word *Santaclaus*. The town's unique name went largely unnoticed until the late 1920s, when Postmaster James Martin began promoting the Santa Claus postmark. The name was changed back to *Santa*

Claus on February 17, 1928. It was then that the Post Office Department decided there would never be another Santa Claus Post Office in the United States, due to the influx of holiday mail. The growing volume of holiday mail became so substantial that it caught the attention of Robert Ripley in 1929, who featured the town's post office in his nationally syndicated *Ripley's Believe It or Not!* cartoon strip.

Learn more about this unique town here: https://santaclausind.org

PROLOGUE

Christmas - 5 Years Earlier

"What should we bake for the fundraiser?"

"Honestly, I think maybe we should do the sugar cutouts and perhaps some brownies. Everyone loves your brownies!"

"And everyone loves those little cookies you make... You know the ones you coat in icing sugar."

"Oh, I didn't know they liked snowballs."

"They sure do. Perhaps we should make those."

"Well, I guess we could. I could drop by after I'm done with my last class tonight. I will bring the ingredients for the cutouts and the snowballs."

"Okay, that sounds good. I'm sure I have the ingredients for the brownies."

My phone pinged with a message, and I stopped rooting through the cupboard and reached for it while Kenzie blabbed on about if I had icing sugar. Careful not to hang up on her, I swiped through the screens on my phone, finally seeing Declan's name. A funny feeling in the pit of my stomach rose as he once again begged me to respond. I cleared the message and placed my phone back on the counter, reached back into the cupboard, and finally found the bag of icing sugar she had been talking about.

"No need to pick up the icing sugar. I found the bag," I called out.

"Awesome. Okay, I will see you about six."

"See you then."

I ended the call with Kenzie, climbed down off the stool, and continued picking at the rotisserie chicken I had picked up from the grocery store. My phone vibrated away on the counter. I already knew it was Declan again, and even though I was angry, I still read every single one of his messages.

Once I finished eating, I sat in the rocking chair beside the Christmas tree in my living room. I sipped on hot cocoa while Christmas carols played in the background, and I stared at the twinkling lights. Tears streamed down my face as the memory of the last time I had seen Declan sat fresh in my mind. I was a mess, and no matter how much I told myself I would be all right, every night for the past two months had ended like this. Declan would beg me for forgiveness for whatever he had done, and I would ignore his pleas.

Any other night I would have been happy to wallow in tears, but tonight wasn't the night for this. Kenzie would be here any minute to bake the cookies for the feed-the-homeless fundraiser. I hadn't told her anything about what had happened over Columbus Day weekend, just that Declan and I had decided to go different paths. It was far from the truth, but it stopped her from asking me questions. Come to think of it, I hadn't told a single person about what had really happened. I'd bottled it up and refused to speak of it again, figuring that would make it better. Yet I still sat here torturing myself by reading every text he had sent me over the past five weeks.

I grabbed a handful of tissues and blew my nose just as the buzzer to my apartment rang. I wiped the tears from my cheeks and glanced at myself in the mirror before I opened the door to let Kenzie in. I just hoped she wouldn't notice all the puffiness under my eyes.

A concerned look quickly replaced the smile she wore on her face when she saw me. She pushed past me, her arms full, and ran into the kitchen, dumping the bags on my small table. She wasted no time pouring herself a glass of wine and turning to me as she leaned against the counter.

"Are you ever going to tell me what happened?"

I shook my head and peeked inside the grocery bags to see what she had brought.

"Come on, Harper, look at yourself. I know that something happened between you and Declan. Why don't you just tell me?"

I took the last mouthful of my hot cocoa and shook my head. "It was nothing. Plus, I already told you we've gone our separate ways, okay. Did you want hot cocoa?"

"I don't believe you," she said, pulling her phone from her pocket. "I'm going to have Devon call Declan and get it out of him."

I shrugged. "Do whatever you feel you have to, but seriously, it's nothing. Let's just bake some cookies and have fun, okay."

Kenzie took one look at me and shoved her phone back into her pocket. "I guess I am just sad that you two aren't together anymore."

I shrugged. "Me too, but let's just forget it, please. We have cookies to bake for charity, and that is more important than some silly relationship that was probably never going to work."

"Of course, it matters." Kenzie said as she wrapped her arms around me and pulled me in for a hug.

We soon covered my kitchen counters with ingredients and bowls as we started baking. That was how I left it with Kenzie. I never told her what had transpired to cause us to go our separate ways because I figured that after a few years it wouldn't matter. Life would go on, I would eventually meet someone, and they would enter my circle of friends. The same would go for Declan. He would meet someone, and he would get a new circle, and I would never have to see him again.

CHAPTER 1

HARPER

The cab drove over the snow-covered roads, and for the first time in a long time, I felt a hint of excitement as we finally passed the welcome sign to Santa Claus, Indiana. It had been a long day of traveling. I had booked the last flight here. It had two layovers and had taken a little over eight hours to get there, when it should have only taken four. I pulled the brochure for Mistletoe Lodge from my bag, along with the invitation to the wedding. I was extremely excited to see Kenzie and Devon.

"Are we almost there?" I asked from the backseat as I glanced down at the invite again.

"Yes, Miss. Just around the corner. You really should check out Santa's Candy Castle while you are here. They have the best hot cocoa."

"I will take that into consideration, thank you," I said as he pulled the cab to a stop.

Mistletoe Lodge was even more beautiful than it had been in the brochure. I looked up at the extensive building from the back of the cab. It was beautifully decorated with white Christmas lights and garland attached too much of the building and gardens that twinkled against the darkness. I smiled, got out of the cab, paid the driver, and walked up the front steps. If I hurried, I could make it in time for the rehearsal dinner, I thought. I instantly sent Kenzie a text letting her know I had finally arrived and was going to be checking in before I shoved my phone back into my pocket.

I struggled with my suitcase up the steps and through the door, but once inside, I stopped and stood looking around the lobby. I brushed the snow from my coat as I stepped to the side to allow a small group of people, all bundled in winter coats, pass out the front door. I smiled at their excitement.

It literally felt as if I stepped into a Christmas movie. They had decorated the lobby for Christmas, garland was hung everywhere and every inch twinkled with little white lights. A large Christmas tree stood by a large stone hearth. I glanced at an elderly couple who sat in front of the fireplace. He was reading, and she was knitting, and I smiled to myself. A sign off to the right of the tree put an even larger smile on my face as I read the words, "Mistletoe Lodge is happy to announce the wedding of Kenzie Butler & Devon Thornton." I was finally here, and even though I was exhausted from the trip, I couldn't wait to celebrate their special day.

I ran my hand through my hair and turned to walk toward the front desk to check in but stopped in my tracks at who I saw. There, dressed in jeans and an expensive-looking sweater, leaning on one elbow texting up a storm, looking sexy as ever, stood Declan Brookes. The feeling of excitement I'd had only moments ago had now been replaced with some emotion I barely recognized.

I could feel a fiery rage building inside of me as he flirted with the girl at the front desk, flashing that sexy smile, showing off those dimples I had once thought were so sexy. Honestly, I'd rather hoped never to lay eyes on him again. What was he was doing here?

Kenzie and Devon had mentioned nothing to me at all about him coming for the wedding. Although, knowing Kenzie, she probably worried that if I knew he was going to be here, I might not show up. Perhaps he wasn't even here for the wedding, I thought. It could just be a coincidence that he was staying in the same small town and same hotel for the weekend. At least, I hoped that was the case. I digested that idea and decided I would just ignore him, but as I stepped forward, Devon came out of the elevator and walked over to Declan. They did the same stupid fist bump thing they always used to do and exchanged some words. Declan's laugh rang through the lobby, and then before I knew it, Devon had disappeared. Guess I could kiss that idea goodbye.

I blew out a breath. It didn't look like Declan was going to leave soon, and I'd have to face the music of sorts. I walked across the lobby toward the front desk when I heard my name. I turned in time to see Kenzie come running towards me. I didn't get any words out because she plowed into me, wrapped her arms around me, and pulled me in for a tight hug.

"You're here. You made it just in time for the rehearsal dinner. I'm so glad you could make it for tonight."

"Told you I would."

"I know, but with your flight being a double layover, I just assumed you'd be late."

Glancing back at the front desk, I silently wished the plane I'd been on had crashed to the ground with me in it instead of having to see Declan again. I was just about to ask her what he was doing here when she grabbed my hand and pulled me in the opposite direction.

"You can check in later. First, you need to see the setup for the rehearsal dinner," she said excitedly.

He stared at me from across the table, then he leaned in and whispered something to Devon, taking his eyes off me. He nodded in response to what Devon had said, and then those dark-blue eyes reverted to me as Devon glanced over at me. I watched as he picked up his fork and shoved a roasted potato into his mouth. Devon leaned in and said something, causing them both to laugh.

He smiled in my direction, but I just rolled my eyes, picked up my wineglass, and turned my attention to something Kenzie was saying.

The high-pitched tone of a spoon tapping on the side of the crystal wineglass pulled all of our attention, and our group quieted.

Kenzie's' mom stood at the head of the table smiling down on everyone. She cleared her throat before speaking. "We are so happy all of you could attend the wedding of Kenzie and Devon. I know some of you have travelled far, but know that both Kenzie and Devon are thrilled to have their closest friends by their sides for their special day," Kenzie's mother said as she turned to look at her husband.

I reached across my plate and picked up my wineglass again, taking a sip of my favorite Moscato. As Alexandra went on talking about her daughter and future son-in-law, I watched Declan Brooks. There were no words to describe how much I hated him and couldn't figure out why the hell Kenzie would think it would be okay to invite him.

As I sat there glaring at him, I felt a sharp jab in my side. I looked over at Kenzie, seeing her eyes bulging. "Stop it," she whispered tight-jawed, so not to interrupt her mother's speech.

"What?" I mouthed back. "I'm not doing anything."

She glanced over at Devon and shook her head and turned back to me. "You don't need to make it so blatantly obvious that you hate him."

I shrugged and went back to drinking my wine, trying to ignore the fact that he was still sitting across from me.

When the speeches were over and we had finished dessert, we all got up to go into the adjoining room to party the night away. I had been the first to take off and was just about to the door when Kenzie called me over to the side.

"Harper, please do me a favor please and don't ruin my wedding."

"What do you mean? Why would you think I would do that?"

"Look, I'm not being a bridezilla or anything. I just don't want you to ruin my big day. It took a lot of planning, and I know your not thrilled about Declan being here."

I blew out a breath. "I promise I won't ruin your big day. It's just so hard seeing him again. How was I supposed to know that Devon still talked to him after all this time? I guess it just would have been nice to have some sort of, oh, I don't know... a warning, maybe."

"I know. Devon kept asking me if I'd told you. I guess I wanted you to be here so bad that I feared you would say no to me if you knew he was going to be the best man."

"Best man?" I asked, shock lining my voice. "You mean he is going to be my partner all day tomorrow?"

"Yes."

I blew out a breath and tried to calm my nerves.

"Look, I wouldn't have done that to you. I would have still come to the wedding. I would have said no to being the maid of honor, if I knew he would be paired with me for all the festivities, but I wouldn't have not come," I bit out, knowing that in a few short hours I would have to be attached to his side for the wedding.

"Are you serious? You are my best friend. I wouldn't have allowed that to happen, but in all fairness to Declan, he is Devon's best friend."

"Perhaps I will talk to him. You know, tell him not to get any idea's, maybe get some closure so I can move on before the wedding."

"No, no way. No closure until after the ceremony tomorrow. Better yet, no closure until we are on our way to the airport for our honeymoon. Then you can get as much closure as you like, as loud as you like, however you would like," she said, raising her eyebrows.

"What is that look supposed to mean?"

"What, you can't be serious. He is as hot as ever. Perhaps you'd like to take him for a spin or something," Kenzie said, jabbing me with her elbow and laughing.

Her attempt at humor wasn't appreciated nor was it funny. There was no way in hell I was doing anything with Declan Brookes, except getting the closure I needed and deserved.

I looked at Kenzie and smiled. "Fine, if I must wait."

"Yes, you must. Now let's go party the night away. It's my last night as a single woman, you know."

I let out a laugh. "You haven't been single since you were sixteen, and it's never stopped you, but let's go."

CHAPTER 2
DECLAN

As the speeches went on, I sat remembering the conversation that I'd had with Devon and Kenzie, when they both warned me to be on my best behavior this weekend. I had told myself repeatedly that it wouldn't be an issue that Harper was there, that I was completely over her, but the second she sat down across from me at the dinner table everything changed. I couldn't keep my eyes off her. She was as beautiful as she'd ever been. Her dark eyes still sparkled and danced when she laughed, and her soft, golden-brown hair, full of lush curls, still looked silken to the touch. The way her dress clung to her curves had me wanting to run my hands all over her body. Then she set her eyes on me, and the beautiful, sexy smile she wore washed away in an instant.

I'd really hoped her response would have been different towards me. It had been years since we'd seen one another, but all she did was glare. I did not understand what had happened between us that caused her to stop talking to me all those years ago. I wanted to know and had begged both Devon and Kenzie to tell me, but neither of them knew either. Once I knew she was coming I had thoughts of perhaps getting back together and then I had finally decided that I wanted closure. Although, now that I'd seen her, I changed my mind. I wanted Harper back.

Once the speeches were finished, I leaned back against my chair and watched as Harper made her way to the adjoining room where all of us could party and hang out for the evening. I was excited she would be there tonight. Maybe we could talk and clear the air between us before tomorrow. Then I watched as Kenzie pulled her aside. I could see her glancing my way every now and again, and I wanted to know what was being said.

"Jesus, man, are you not over her yet?" Devon said, punching me in the arm.

"Man, I thought I could do this, but, honestly, no, I'm not over her. I thought we would have been together forever. I figured we would have been married by now with a couple of kids. Instead, one morning she just stopped answering my calls and texts and blocked me on all social media. It was almost as if all those years we had of being together meant nothing to her."

"Don't say that, man. Harper isn't like that."

"Really? You think not? I guess I find it so hard because I really don't understand why she did that."

"I don't either, man, but I am sure she had her reasons."

"Maybe I should try to talk to her over the weekend, you know, clear the air."

"Ha, that's funny."

"What is? That I want some closure or perhaps another chance?"

"Please don't take this the wrong way, but don't plan to do that tonight or tomorrow. Seriously, you do anything at all to ruin this wedding for Kenzie..."

"Hey, I will do nothing to ruin your wedding. It's your day too. You are my best friend."

Devon chuckled. "Dude, if this were my day, we'd be taking our vows with a judge in a five-minute ceremony at city hall, and then all us men would hang out at the local bar, eat wings, and watch hockey. Fuck all this shit." He said gesturing to the table.

I laughed. Devon was right, it was over the top. Yet, no matter how over the top it was, I just hoped he realized how lucky he really was.

"I guess we should get in there."

We both got up from our seats and stretched. I pushed my chair in and glanced over to where Kenzie and Harper had been standing. Harper now had her arm around Kenzie and both disappeared into the other room.

If I thought I was going to talk to her tonight, I was mistaken. The girls were all huddled over in a corner, talking and laughing, like they would have done at a high school dance, while we men played pool and drank beer.

While I waited for the guys to take their turns, I watched her dancing, smiling and laughing. I should have been the one to make her smile like that.

When the song was over, she placed her empty glass on a table, whispered something to Kenzie, and walked out of the room. The girls made their way over to the bar to get more drinks, and I took this as my opportunity to speak to Harper alone.

I excused myself, saying I needed to use the washroom, and took off in the same direction as Harper.

Instead of using the washroom, I sat down in a chair outside of the bathroom and waited for her to exit.

It hadn't even been three minutes when the woman's washroom door opened, and Harper came walking out. I stood and smiled, but instead of being greeted with a smile, she greeted with a scowl and avoided my eyes.

"Harper, it's good to see you again."

"I have nothing to say to you, Declan," she bit out and went to step around me, but I blocked her.

"Aren't you the least bit happy to see me?"

She let out a huff and crossed her arms across her chest. "Look, I am here to see my best friends get married. I didn't come here to see you or reconnect with you. Truthfully, if I had known you were going to be here, I probably wouldn't be."

"Whoa, Harper." Her words stung, as did the look of death she was giving me. I realized in those seconds that whatever I had done had hurt her permanently. I just wished I knew what it was.

"Declan, do me a favor. Leave me be this weekend. I will be cordial to you tomorrow because I have no choice but to be, but otherwise, I have nothing to say to you. Now please excuse me."

She didn't wait for a response. She pushed past me, pulled the door open, and re-entered the party area. I took a minute to compose myself and swallow her words before I made my way back to the boys.

CHAPTER 3

HARPER

After the run-in with Declan outside of the washroom, I had excused myself from the party. I needed to clear my head, so I returned to my room and ordered a pot of tea. I changed into my pajamas, opened the curtains and sat watching the snow lazily fall to the ground while I sipped on the hot tea. I thought back to the night that ended my relationship with Declan. It was ridiculous that after all these years I was still hung up on what I'd seen that night. I should have been over it and thought I was until I walked in and saw him.

When I was finally tucked under the covers, I tossed and turned. The words I had spewed at Declan outside of the washroom were running through my mind. There was really no reason for me to be so mean, but apparently the wound was still raw, and I felt as if this wedding was just pouring salt into it.

I'd barely slept and now I stood in Kenzie's room, peering into the mirror at the dark circles that were still visible under my makeup.

"Can you help me for a second?" Kenzie asked, coming into the bathroom holding her dress up. "I can't get it done up, and everyone else is getting their makeup or hair done."

My hair had already been finished, and I stood half-dressed looking at Kenzie's pleading eyes. "Turn around."

She did as I asked, and I buttoned up the back of her dress.

"Do you remember how we used to plan our weddings when we were in high school?" Kenzie questioned as I pulled the top of her dress tight.

I thought back to the countless hours we used to spend doing that. We would flip through magazines and surf the web tirelessly for ideas, arguing over what one another had found. I'd had my entire wedding to Declan planned out, right down to the type of flowers and cake I would have at my ceremony. Kenzie had done the same. However, she had stolen the style of dress I had wanted, but it was okay because, truthfully, the sweetheart neckline, fit and flare style looked better on her than it would have on me anyway. I stood back, looking her over and adjusting the back of her dress.

"I do. Seems like a waste of time now though." I chuckled. "Hours agonizing over roses or peonies in pink or red. Red velvet or chocolate cake. I don't even know what I was thinking with this style of dress though."

"I'm sorry I stole your dress idea. It was always my favorite."

"It's all good. There is no one knocking down my door to marry me anytime soon. I'd rather see it go to good use because you look gorgeous," I said, winking.

"Just so you know, I went with vanilla cake." We both burst into laughter as I stood up and took another look at my best friend.

The four of us had always been so intertwined in everything we had done. Honestly, even though Declan and I were no longer together, I was glad that the four of us got to share one of our special days together.

"Are you going to be okay today?" Kenzie asked as I fastened the last clip on the back of her dress.

"Of course. Why wouldn't I be?"

"I know he approached you last night. I know you went to bed because you were angry."

"I wasn't angry," I bit out a little too harshly, causing Kenzie to hold her hands up.

I took a deep breath before speaking again. "Listen, I am fine. Yes, he approached me last night, but honestly, I am over anything Declan Brookes could ever offer me and have been for a long time." I paused. "And just so you know, I went to bed because I was exhausted."

Kenzie stopped me from fussing over her dress anymore and looked me in the eye. "I'm sorry he hurt you."

I could feel the tears starting to build behind my eyes and held my hand up to stop Kenzie from saying any more.

"This is ridiculous. My God, it's been years, Kenzie. So, stop with all this Declan and Harper talk. This is your day, your weekend, and it's almost time, so let's get you married."

Just as I finished saying those words, a knock on the door startled both of us.

"Flowers are here!" Jordan yelled from the other side of the door.

Two hours later, we'd just finished the pictures and we stood in the hallway outside of the chapel doors. We could hear the voices of the guests as they chatted amongst themselves.

"Are you ready?" I whispered to Kenzie.

She glanced up at me with nervous eyes. I placed my hand on her arm, waiting for her answer. Finally, she nodded, and I couldn't help but laugh as I wrapped my arms around her and gave her a hug. "It will be okay, right?" she whispered in my ear.

I pulled back and looked her in the eyes. "Girl, you have nothing to worry about. I honestly cannot think of someone who would be better for you, the two of you are made for one another. You look stunning, and I know Devon is going to fall at your feet when he sees you."

"Thank you, Harper. Thank you for being here today."

I leaned in and hugged her just as the music began to play inside the chapel, and the wedding coordinator worked quickly at getting us all in our places just in time for the doors to open. A hush fell over the crowd and the two flower girls began their walk down the aisle, followed by two of the bridesmaids. The wedding coordinator nodded at me when it was my turn.

"Put a smile on your face when you walk down that aisle," Kenzie practically hissed behind me.

I looked back at her and smiled and then turned getting myself ready to face the crowd. Holding tightly to my bouquet, I stepped into the doorway of the chapel and took my first steps down the aisle. At first, I was afraid to look up, but when I did, the first person my eyes landed on was Declan.

He stood there in his tux, muscular hands clasped in front of him, looking handsome as ever. I swallowed hard again as his blue eyes washed over me. I could feel my body heating under his stare. No matter how angry at him I found myself, a sense of sadness came over me. This would be the closest that Declan ever came to seeing me walk down an aisle.

CHAPTER 4

Declan

We stood inside the little room at the front of the chapel. The guys had been a rowdy bunch this morning, but I had been rather quiet. The only thing on my mind was the conversation with Harper last night. I had spent most of the early evening last night agonizing over what could have caused the breakup between Harper and me all those years ago, instead of having a good time with my friends. This morning wasn't much different.

When I had seen her sneak out of the room last night, I had made the poor decision to approach her because, somehow, I figured opening up the lines of communication might make today a little easier for the both of us. I'd hoped that she would have shed some light on what had caused her to suddenly hate me, but I had been wrong. I had gotten the opposite reaction to what I had been hoping for.

"You have the rings, right?" Devon asked, leaning up against the wall beside me.

"For the hundredth time, yes," I said, putting my hand into my pocket to feel the velvet box.

"Sorry, man, just nervous I guess."

"It's fine."

"You all right?"

"I guess."

"Where did you disappear to last night?"

"I tried to talk to Harper."

Devon looked at me, shaking his head. "Please don't do anything that will cause a scene tonight."

"I won't. I just thought clearing the air with her would make today easier somehow." I shrugged. "But it ended up doing the opposite."

"You're sure the rings are in the box, right," he said, reverting to his original question.

"Yes, I am sure," I gritted.

"All right, geez I'm sorry," he said, moving over to the rest of the guys.

Devon shouldn't have been worried about the rings. He should have been more concerned that I was going to corner Kenzie tonight after a few beers and demand to know what I had done. She must have known something about why Harper wasn't speaking to me. It not only drove me nuts wondering what had happened between us, but it also bothered me to know that she was still harbouring so much anger that she wouldn't speak to me.

I quickly averted my thoughts when the wedding coordinator appeared and signaled for us to take out spots at the front of the chapel. I followed Devon as he headed out the door and took my spot beside him.

We'd barely been standing there looking out at all the guests when the music started and the doors to the chapel opened. We watched as the flower girls made their way down the aisle, dropping rose petals along the way. Then came the bridesmaids, smiling to the people in the audience.

I averted my gaze to the floor, and when I glanced to the door again, Harper rounded the corner. My heart rate sped up the second I saw her. She looked gorgeous in the form-fitting blue dress, showing off all her curves. Her eyes were locked on the floor, but the second she lifted her head, her eyes locked with mine.

At first, I imagined that she was walking down that aisle to join me at my side, and my heart filled with hope. Then the realization hit that this was the only way I would ever get to see her walk down an aisle. The next time she would walk down the aisle would be to her future husband, which should have been me. A streak of jealousy ran through me at the thought.

As I watched her make her way down the aisle, her eyes never left mine. It was almost as if we were in sync for the first time in five years. She finally took her place, peeling her eyes away from mine to look down to the door where Kenzie appeared and started walking down the aisle with her father. A hush came over the crowd, and I looked back to Harper in time to see a tear slip down her cheek. I missed the entire thing, because no matter how hard I tried, I could not take my eyes off my girl.

Twenty minutes later, we stood, the priest speaking to both Kenzie and Devon. I stood there completely in my own world, staring over at Harper, dreaming of what could have been. I jumped when I felt the guy behind me subtly jam his fist into my back. Forgetting where I was, I just about to turn to give him a piece of my mind when I noticed Devon standing there staring at me.

"The rings," he mouthed, tight-jawed.

Not knowing how I had missed the cue, I drove my hand into my pocket and pulled the box out, opening it and handing him the ring. I closed the box quietly and shoved it back into my pocket and glanced over to Harper. She rolled her eyes at me, softly smiled, and turned her attention back to our friends as they recited their vows and exchanged rings.

In a matter of minutes, the guests broke into applause, and Devon and Kenzie shared their first kiss as a married couple and then turned to the guests while they announced Mr. And Mrs. Devon Thornton.

I felt a sense of relief as both Kenzie and Devon took off down the aisle. I looked over to see Harper step into the aisle, pausing while waiting for me to join her. As I stepped into the aisle, I signaled for her to lace her arm through mine and she did so hesitantly. The second her arm connected with mine, I felt a wave of electricity flow through me.

"You look beautiful," I whispered as we took our first uncomfortable steps down the aisle and out of the chapel.

She said nothing in return, just smiled at the guests. This really was the closest I would ever come to marrying her.

CHAPTER 5

HARPER

"Good afternoon, ladies and gentlemen," Declan said, tipping his glass to the crowd of guests who sat at their tables.

I rolled my eyes as he tried to get everyone's attention. Finally, the room quieted down, and he stood there looking out into the crowd.

"Before I begin, I just want to say, I asked Devon before I started writing if there was anything I should not say, and he said no. So, Kenzie, whatever I'm about to say, just remember this is really his fault." Devon and Kenzie both laughed.

"I'd like to start by pointing out how amazing Kenzie looks today—every bit the beautiful bride. As for Devon? Well, what can one do with the mess he is?"

The entire crowd started laughing. I just sat there, a displeased look on my face, and took a sip of my wine.

"You know, I was always taught that if you have nothing nice to say, say nothing at all, but in this case, it needs to be said. Devon, he tries hard, and this is Devon... trying...hard...And his personality...it's great too. It really makes up for everything that's going on up there in the face area."

The guests once again broke out in laughter. I picked up my wineglass and emptied the remaining contents from it, signaling for a refill from a nearby server. This speech was Declan, through and through.

"Okay, so let me introduce myself. My name is Declan, and I've known Devon since the second grade. I am his oldest, most handsome, most personable, most... okay, I'm his friend. I met Devon when we were both seven. It's really easy to imagine seven-year-old Devon. He had the same haircut and the same brief smile—you know, the one that says he is always pleased with himself. When he smiles, it's as if he's thinking back on his many accomplishments. From being president of the student body in middle school to getting into and graduating from Stanford at the top of his class. Today counts as one of his biggest accomplishments to date—committing to a woman like Kenzie. Today, you lead the way, to becoming a man and starting a family. Don't mess it up."

Declan went on for another fifteen minutes, another two glasses of wine for me. I was grateful I had done my speech first because I wouldn't have been able to do it now. The second Declan had finished, I excused myself from the table and headed out the side door to the patio.

The blast of frigid air hit me the second I opened the door, and I could breathe again. I pulled the door shut behind me, drowning out the voices and the music and walked across the snow-covered patio, crossing my arms over my chest.

I leaned against the railing and looked out over the property. I could still hear his words, "Don't mess this up." They sounded funny coming from his lips. How could he give that advice when he had been the one fully responsible for messing us up?

Why had I promised Kenzie I wouldn't say anything? I had a ton to say to him, and it all started with demanding to know why he had done what he had done. I bit my lip. I would keep my promise to her, even if it killed me. I already knew that if I started with him right now it wouldn't end well, and it would ultimately ruin her wedding. That was the last thing I wanted to do. She shouldn't have to suffer because I was hurting.

I leaned against the cold railing, fighting off a shiver, and did my best to clear my mind. I heard the MC announce the first dance between the bride and groom and wished I could have been in there to watch. I'd been standing there about five minutes when I heard the click of a door behind me and loud music poured out onto the patio. I turned in time to see Declan step out onto the patio, smile shyly at me, before he shut the door behind him, the music quieting considerably.

"Everything okay? What are you doing out here?" he asked like he had a right to know before taking a few steps towards me.

I let out the breath I was holding. It must have been the wine because I didn't have it in my heart to be mean to him. "Just clearing my head and freezing," I said, crossing my bare arms over my chest and rubbing them with my hands, trying to warm myself.

"Here, hold on." With a quick flick, Declan had undone the button on his suit jack and slipped out of it, wrapping me in it. "That better?"

The scent of his cologne sent a tingle through me, and the warmth from his body was welcoming and instantly warmed me as I slid my bare arms into the arms of his jacket. "Yes. Thank you."

He was quiet, and we just stood and looked at one another for what felt like a long time, and then he cleared his throat. "It's been a while," he said, his eyes falling from my eyes to my lips.

"Yes, it has."

"We really should talk," he said.

"No, Declan, not now." I didn't trust myself enough, I didn't trust that I wouldn't get angry and cause a scene.

He glanced at me at my abrupt answer and was about to say something when the next song played. From the first two notes, I knew immediately what song it was. Richard Marx had always been one of my favorite singers, and his song "Right Here Waiting" had always been known as "our song." I knew the longer this song played, the more the memories and feelings would flow, and that I needed to get inside and away from Declan Brookes. Instead, his eyes met mine, and he held his hand out for me to take.

"How about a dance? Just for old times sake?"

I hesitated. I didn't know what to say. This song was one we danced to at every high-school dance we'd attended, and instantly my mind went right back to every one of those memories. The memories of being held in his powerful arms and feeling the safest I think

I had ever felt in my life. I remembered resting my head on his shoulder, nuzzling my nose into the crook of his neck, and inhaling his scent.

"Just one dance, Harper. I promise not to bite."

I looked into his eyes, I wanted to feel his arms around me and remember what it felt like to be held by him again, no matter how angry I still was. Hesitantly, I placed my hand into his. He pulled me into his arms and started dancing, holding me close as the song played. I leaned in, rested my head on his shoulder, and I couldn't help but breathe in the musky scent of his cologne. As the song played and he held me securely in his arms, he lightly whispered the words of the song into my ear, just as he always had.

I closed my eyes, trying hard to fight the feelings that were rising in me. I was somewhere between wishing we were still together and fighting to remember how angry I was with him, but the longer I stood, him holding me in his arms, the longer the second feeling was waning and the first was rising.

"Wow, did you see that shooting star?" he whispered in my ear.

I had seen the star shoot across the sky, but instead of letting him know, I shook my head no.

"Remember how we always used to wish on them?"

"That in order for the wishes to come true we had to whisper our wish to one another."

"Yes. That is it," he whispered, while holding me in his arms, while the music still played. He pulled me tighter against him and whispered, "Well, I have one more wish, Harper. I want you back."

A chill ran through me at his confession. I pulled my head back and stared into his eyes, and as if in slow motion, he leaned in and brushed his lips against mine. When he pulled back to look at me again, I couldn't help but allow myself to step in and kiss him back.

I closed my eyes and met his lips. I, too, wished for something, only I never whispered it. I wished that somehow, in my heart, I could find a way to forgive Declan Brookes. As I leaned in to meet his lips again, I knew I needed to figure out how to move forward, so I could invite Declan back into my life for good.

CHAPTER 6
DECLAN

Our lips had parted, and we stood there staring at one another when the door to the patio opened, music and loud laughter forcing us apart instantly. Harper turned to look out over the snowy landscape as a few people stepped out onto the patio and made their way over to the railing, completely ignoring the fact that we had been in the middle of a private moment.

I stepped up behind Harper and placed my hands on her shoulders. "Did you want to go back inside?" I questioned.

"Might be good idea," she said, removing my jacket from her shoulders and handing it back to me.

She walked ahead of me, pulling the door open and stepping into the crowded room. I pulled the door closed behind us. Harper immediately headed over to her table and drank down the contents of her wine glass. I slowly approached her and was just about to say something when I felt a tap on my shoulder. I turned around to see Kenzie and Devon standing in front of me.

"Declan, thank you so much for all your kind words." Kenzie said, leaning in to give me a hug.

"No problem, Kenzie. It was my pleasure."

"No, really, the ending of the speech was so heartfelt, oh and Harper, you're my best friend. Your words were just so meaningful," she said, throwing her arms around Harper and pulling her in for a hug. "I wish you guys had never broken up. You both should be together forever."

I glanced to Harper, a look of sadness falling in her eyes as she looked to me. "All right, well, thanks for everything, guys. We are off to bed," Devon said, trying to pry Kenzie off Harper. "She needs to sleep it off."

Kenzie turned and looked to Devon and started laughing. "I don't know what you are talking about. I'm not drunk. Everything I said is true. They need to realize they are perfect for one another."

"You need to realize it's time for bed now," Devon said, looking at both of us and mouthing an apology.

"I'm heading up now too. I have a long day of travel ahead of me tomorrow," Harper said, giving both Kenzie and Devon one more hug.

"All right, let's go," Devon said, once again prying Kenzie off Harper. They were about halfway to the exit when Kenzie slipped out of Devon's arms and ran back over in our direction.

"My God, I just noticed you two are standing side by side in the same room and not fighting. I also saw you both slip out the side door. Are you both going to get back together?"

I glanced to Harper and she to me, neither of us saying anything.

"Don't fuck up my wedding, Brookes," Kenzie slurred, a hiccup finding its way out, causing her to laugh and cover her mouth.

"Come on, Kenzie, let's get you up to bed," Devon said, grabbing her and trying to turn her around, once again mouthing an apology.

"Whatever you do, keep it down," she said in a hushed whisper as Devon pulled her away.

I watched as he guided her out of the reception and into the hallway to wait for an elevator. Hopefully, they didn't have to wait long, I thought to myself.

Harper looked at me, placing her glass down on the table, a laugh escaping her.

"What's so funny?" I asked.

"Nothing, just Kenzie," she said, glancing at her watch, letting me know that it must be getting late for her.

"Are you really going to turn in?"

"Yes, I think so."

"Would you like to get some dessert first?" I asked, nodding to the dessert table.

"Um, I probably shouldn't. I could go for a tea or coffee though."

"Why don't you come back to my room. We will get a tea or coffee and talk."

Harper glanced around the room, looking a little nervous at my suggestion. "I don't know, Declan."

"I could come to your room if that makes you more comfortable. Or perhaps the lounge in the lobby."

She bit the corner of her bottom lip and looked at me. "All right, I guess you can come to my room if you like."

Without another word, she took a couple of steps

and turned to see if I was following her. I was a little shocked at her response, but I followed her anyway.

We got into the elevator and each stood on opposite sides. We said nothing, and when the bell notified us we were on the ninth floor, I allowed Harper to exit first, following behind her down the hall until she stopped outside of room number fifteen. She inserted a key, opened the door, and walked in, holding the door for me.

She walked into the room and pulled her heels off, dropping each one to the floor. I closed the door and turned in time to watch as she unclipped her hair, allowing her soft, sexy curls to fall. I instantly wanted to grab her and run my fingers through the mess of curls.

"Tea or coffee?" she questioned as she picked up the phone.

"Coffee please."

She quickly placed the order and then hung up the phone, sitting down on the end of the bed, pulling her foot up to massage it.

"Here, let me," I said, stepping further into the room and sitting on the chair across from the bed. She looked at me as if I had lost my mind, but she placed her foot in my hand.

I dug into the ball of her foot with my thumb, and her eyes closed instantly, a soft moan escaping her lips.

"I forgot how good your hands were," she mumbled as she leaned back on her arms.

I said nothing—I couldn't—but the raging hard-on behind my zipper reminded me I was still as attracted to her as I was years ago. She slipped the first foot out of my hands and replaced it with the other, repeating the same actions.

A knock on the door caused me to stop. She pulled her foot from my lap and walked over to the door, bringing in the tray of tea and coffee and setting it on the table in the corner. She poured us each a mug and handed me mine. She sat back on the end of the bed and sipped her tea, holding the mug with both hands. We both sat there in uncomfortable silence, staring at one another as we sipped our drinks.

"What are we doing here, Harper?" I questioned, placing my mug down on the desk as I watched her run her fingers through her hair. "It's not exactly a secret that you hate me."

Harper averted her eyes from mine and looked down to the mug in her hand. "This is closure, Declan."

I nodded and glanced around her room. "Is that what you want? Closure?"

"You have no clue," she whispered.

"I think I have some idea, Harper. I was there for

that kiss. It sure didn't feel like you wanted closure. It also didn't feel like closure when you invited me back here."

Harper stood and placed her mug on the table. I stood, setting my mug down, and watched as Harper walked over to me and placed her hands on my chest. "It's what I want, Declan. It's what I need to move on," she said, standing in front of me, biting her lower lip as she looked into my eyes.

I knew that when Harper bit the corner of her lower lip, she was doubting herself. It had always been a tell-tale sign.

She met my eyes. I took a chance and ran my hands over her hips and up her back, looking down into her eyes. She stepped forward into me, and I stepped back until we were only inches from the wall.

"If closure is what you truly want, then I will give you what you want."

Instead of answering me, she leaned in and met my lips, shoving me up against the wall. Her kiss got harder, and more intense, as her hands made their way around my neck. I wrapped my arms around her waist and spun her around, pushing her up against the wall. I gripped both of her hands and raised them above her head, holding them there while I assaulted her mouth.

She let out a low, throaty moan as I gripped her ass with my free hand and ground myself against her. She pulled her arms from my grasp and began working at the buttons on my shirt, I pulled the zipper down on the back of her dress

Within seconds, she had my shirt open and was pushing it off my shoulders. It hung from the waist of my pants as my fingers pulled the straps of her dress off her shoulders. I peeled that dress off her body inch by inch, my lips exploring every part of her body as I went.

She didn't hesitate, her fingers found the button on my pants, then the zipper, and then before I knew it, both my pants and boxers were in a pile, around my ankles. She pulled her lips away from my mouth and looked me in the eye before she slowly kneeled in front of me. I couldn't help but watch as she took my cock in her hand, gripping me just firmly enough, and ran her hand down my shaft. I tipped my head back and let out a throaty moan. When I looked back down at her, she surprised me by bringing her tongue to the head of my cock. One soft little lick was all it took, and she brought me completely to my knees when she sucked my cock into her mouth.

"Harper, fuck, you've got to stop, baby," I gritted out as I looked down and met her eyes.

She continued sucking me until I pulled myself away from her and stood her up; I kissed her hard, pushing her against the wall. Gripping her ass, I wrapped her legs around my waist, and turning her toward the closest bed, I dropped her onto the mattress. With her legs spread, I kneeled between them and lined myself up with her entrance and slowly pushed inside of her.

She raked her fingers across my back as I buried myself in her repeatedly, slow and deep at first, then hard and fast. I loved the sounds she was making and could feel my orgasm building fast, so I slowed myself down again, back to the slow, deep, and steady pace.

I could feel her body tightening around me, could feel the tension in all her muscles as I continued that pace. I met her lips and kissed her as she came, muting her moans, as I felt my orgasm build and emptied myself inside of her.

I lay there for a moment, catching my breath before I raised myself up and looked down into her eyes. Neither of us said anything, and I rolled off her and collapsed onto the bed beside her. We both lay there quietly, breathing hard for a few minutes. As I ran over everything that had gone on throughout the evening, I realized that I had missed so much about her. I also realized that no one had ever compared to her. Not even the women I had dated for three years after her could compare to Harper.

I ran my hand over my face and was about to get up when Harper rolled onto her side and rested her head on my chest. She let out a yawn and placed her hand on my chest. I almost froze as she curled into my side. I placed my arm around her, pulled her in close, reached up and shut the light off, and held onto the girl I had been missing for all these years.

CHAPTER 7

HARPER

Declan was still sound asleep when I tip-toed out of my own room well before the sun came up and went down to the lobby to get some air. I wandered the halls of the main floor of the hotel, and then sat down in front of that immense fireplace in the lobby. I leaned back into the over-sized chair and looked up at the twinkling lights of the Christmas tree.

I didn't understand how last night had even happened. When I had seen him in the lobby at first, I had sworn to myself that I was going to hate him to the ends of the earth, but then I found myself in his arms. As he held me outside on that patio, the more my body, mind, and heart betrayed me. Then when we had gotten into the quiet of my room, alone, where I had planned on finishing that closure conversation, all hell broke loose. The more I was near him, the more something came over me.

"Harper? What are you doing up so early?" I heard a familiar voice say and twisted to see Kenzie walking over to the free chair beside me.

"What are you doing up?" I questioned, glancing at my watch.

"Heartburn. Drinking as much as I did does that to you." She smiled and sat down next to me and pulled out a package of antacids from the tiny bag she was carrying. "Are you okay?"

"Yes, of course. Why?"

"Well, normal people are still asleep at four in the morning. Plus, I've known you for a long time. You don't get up this early unless something is bothering you. So, spill it."

I sat there staring at the tree trying to figure out what to say, or better yet how to say it, without being angry with myself. It wasn't the fact that I had slept with

Declan. It was that I had let myself down and went against what I said I would never do, which was give him another chance.

"It's Declan, isn't it?" Kenzie asked, placing her hand on my knee.

I turned and met my friend's eyes, tears building in mine. I shook my head yes.

"Perhaps you should give the guy another chance. Hear him out, instead of harboring all this anger you're holding onto."

If only she knew, I thought to myself. I had never told Kenzie exactly what had happened and wondered that if perhaps I had things might be different. I had just told her we had broken up after I had returned from that Columbus Day weekend and asked her never to mention him in my presence again.

"Anyway, I am going to go back to my room. Get some rest and seriously talk to him."

Kenzie leaned over and hugged me tightly and headed off toward her room.

"Kenzie, wait a minute."

Kenzie walked back over and sat down. "What is it?"

"Um, if you caught Devon kissing someone else, what would you do?"

"I don't think you'd want to know." Kenzie laughed to herself.

"I'm serious. I don't mean now. I mean when we were younger."

"I'd confront him."

I nodded, growing quiet again.

"Is that what happened?"

I blew out a breath and nodded, clasping my hands together in my lap.

"That's why you ended things with him, because you caught him kissing someone?"

"Yes. It was on Columbus Day weekend. I arrived at his dorm and he was there with another girl. I watched the entire thing."

"You never asked him about it?"

"No, I ran, he didn't even know I was going to be there."

"Girl, you need to talk to him. You should have talked to him years ago, but it's not too late. Don't take your second chance away."

Kenzie leaned in and pulled me in for a hug, then she got up and headed back to her room. I sat there for another half hour thinking about what she said before I decided to head back to my room.

I'd quietly entered my room and ducked into the bathroom where I took a hot shower, and now I stood in front of the mirror, wrapped in my bathrobe, looking at my reflection. I had just finished putting on a couple of coats of mascara when I heard a knock on the door. He really should have left already, I thought to myself. I put the cap back on my mascara and threw it in my bag and pulled the door open.

Declan wasted no time. He pulled me in for a good-morning kiss, and my body told me to go for it. My head, however, didn't. I wasn't angry at him any longer, but angry at myself because I had acted on emotion instead of confronting him and giving him a chance to explain. As soon as our lips parted, I pulled away and looked at him.

"I thought you would have left already," I bit out, looking down at his half-dressed body. He still had the body of that eighteen-year-old football player, only more muscular, and I blushed when I realized he had followed my eyes.

"Well, good morning to you too," he said as I pushed my way past him and walked to my suitcase, neatly folding my dress from yesterday and placing it on top of the rest of the clothing.

"As much as I enjoyed last night, something is on my mind, and I need to know, do you still want this to be closure?"

I looked into his blue eyes, all the hurt coming right

back to the surface. "Yes, Declan, I really think that would be for the best."

"Harper, I don't understand. Why?"

"Don't play stupid, Declan. You know. Don't pretend that you don't."

"Harper, I have no idea what you are talking about. I don't understand what happened all those years ago that caused you to walk away from me."

"Let me give you a hint. Do you remember Columbus Day weekend, 2014?"

"Yeah, how could I not? I was missing you so, and honestly thought we were closer than ever. We had spent all that time calling, texting, and face timing, and even though we were thousands of miles apart, I felt as if you were with me every day. I remember suggesting that I come to you or you to me or even that we meet up between our schools, but you insisted you couldn't. You had some project due."

"That's right, but let me enlighten you. The last time I spoke to you before that weekend, you sounded so down on the phone. It worried me. I mean, you were an all-star football player in high school, but only third string in college. I knew you were not only suffering with that but with your classes, and you hated that guy you had for a roommate. I had just read a few articles related to suicide and was so afraid for you. So, after I got off the phone with you on the Wednesday, I decided I would surprise you. I took a cab to the airport, hopped on a plane, and booked a hotel for us for the long weekend, all with the money I had saved up from tutoring."

"What? You were there?"

"Yes, I showed up at your dorm that Friday to surprise you, only the surprise was on me. I found you in the common room, kissing another girl."

"You saw it?"

"I did, and I didn't make a scene. I didn't say a word. Instead, I left with my heart in my throat and spent the rest of the weekend in the hotel trying to decide what I should do. After a good long cry, I spent my time sightseeing alone, until my flight left on Sunday night. When I got home, I unfriended and blocked you on all social media."

I watched as a look settled on his face, a look that told me he knew the exact moment that I was talking about.

"So, you remember?"

"Yeah, but it wasn't what you think."

"Really?"

"Yes, really. There were parties, all kinds of activities to take part in that weekend. I wasn't interested in any of them. That Friday, I tried calling you in the afternoon, but your phone went straight to voicemail. You never didn't answer, and I imagined the worst."

"I was on a flight, how was I going to answer you?"

"I didn't know that, and I was angry that you hadn't responded. Somehow, my roommate and his girlfriend talked me into going to some frat party. I ended up doing a couple keg stands and stumbled back to dorms, landing in the common area and not my room, like I had planned. There I met this girl, and we exchanged dating stories. She was going through something like us and was feeling down. I thought that perhaps talking with her would help not only her but me, but the next thing I knew, she leaned in and kissed me. It was the beer mixed with sheer stupidity. Regardless, I stopped it pretty much as soon as it started and explained to her I had a girlfriend whom I loved."

"Yeah, that is easy to say now."

"Harper, I planned on telling you. I went back to my room and texted you for the entire weekend. I felt so guilty, but you never gave me a chance. I called you every day for weeks, but when I figured out you had blocked me, I resorted to texting, and still nothing. I had no clue why you weren't speaking to me."

"Well, now you know why." I closed my eyes, fighting back tears and then turned to him, "Just so you know, I received every text you sent, but every time one appeared all I could do was cry. Declan, when I saw you with her, my heart shattered into a million pieces. I didn't know what to do."

"Harper, can you ever forgive me?"

Declan kneeled in front of me and brushed a loose strand of hair out of my face, his hand resting on my cheek.

I had wished for this, wished silently that I could find it in my heart to forgive him, but my heart still hurt. I had never thought I would walk in on him with another girl. I had thought we would be together forever.

"These kinds of things take time."

"But you've had five years. Actually, it been a little over five years since that night. Surely, it's easier now."

I looked into his blue eyes—blue eyes that were begging me for forgiveness and another chance. I could tell that whatever had happened that night hadn't been done with ill intent, but still I couldn't just cave.

"Really, you think it's easier now. It was easier until you showed up here. I don't know, Declan. I didn't know the entire story. I just got the apology. I need time. Fresh time to digest everything."

I watched as Declan nodded, then stood up and looked down at me again. "I will let you have all the time you need. We have brunch in an hour. I am going to get ready. I'll come back and pick you up."

"Really, it's unnecessary. I can just meet you and everyone else downstairs."

"Give me forty minutes," he said, glancing at his watch and heading for the door.

As soon as the door clicked shut, I lay back on the bed and searched my heart. I needed to search myself to see if I could forgive him for everything, and I was leaning towards yes, considering how I felt last night in his arms.

CHAPTER 8

DECLAN

"Thank you for the mimosa," Harper said as we walked back from the restaurant.

"You're welcome."

"And thank you for the dessert. How did you ever remember that apple crisp was my favorite?"

Harper had been sitting looking over the dessert menu for almost ten minutes. I knew she had been eying that. She hadn't changed one bit. She had told me once that she always ordered the yogurt and fresh fruit because it made her feel less guilty after having a carb-laden meal. So, instead of allowing her to torture herself, I slipped the menu from her hands and ordered for her. Her eyes had lit up when the server set the full bowl of apple crisp, complete with vanilla ice cream in front of her.

"Are you going to tell me how you remembered?"

"The same way I remembered that mimosas were your favorite. There really isn't anything that I don't remember about you, Harper. You were my first genuine love and, honestly, if I had my way, you'd be my last."

"Declan..."

I held my hand up to stop her from saying anything. "No, Harper, listen. I know I've messed up, but now I at least know you saw me mess up. I accept that I am going to have to earn back your trust and your heart. It's not going to happen overnight, so no matter how long it takes, I won't give up, and even if it never happens, well, at least I can say that I tried."

I was fairly sure I saw a tear in Harper's eyes as she looked in the opposite direction. I said nothing more on the subject. Instead, I took her hand in mine and we walked through the gently falling snow back to the hotel.

We stepped inside the lobby and I glanced at the clock. It was almost one. "Did you want to share a cab to the airport?

Harper nodded. "What time does your flight leave?"

"I fly out about six. It was the only flight I could get after Devon and Kenzie were already gone. Otherwise, I wouldn't have gotten to say goodbye. What about you?"

"Same."

"Okay, so we will have an airport dinner together then. Sound good?"

Harper nodded. "I'm going to get my things." She had walked halfway across the lobby and then turned and made her way back to me. She leaned in and kissed me gently on the cheek without saying a word and then wandered off toward her room.

We both stood and watched Devon and Kenzie board their plane for their honeymoon. The other guests in the wedding party had gone, which just left Harper and me. She wandered over and sat down beside her luggage; the smile disappearing from her lips.

"What is it?" I asked, sitting down next to her and

looking at my watch. We still had almost three hours until our planes were to begin boarding.

"I just hope they have a good time."

"I'm sure they will. We will too. I spotted an Island Grill back there."

"Oh really. That used to be—"

"You're favorite. It was mine too, in case you've forgotten."

"Well, let's go. I haven't had their food in ages. They closed their restaurant in Seattle a little over two years ago." Harper said, grabbing the handle of her bag and standing up.

We sat up against the window in the restaurant, sipping on a drink, when the server dropped our dessert down in front of us.

"So, what are your plans when you get back home?" I asked, digging his fork into the lava cake in front of me.

"I guess I will have to get a Christmas tree before all the lots sell out. I also have a series of meetings to get through at the ad agency before the holidays. I had to reschedule everything because of the wedding. What about you?"

"I get to find out if I got my promotion. I've been waiting to hear from the airline, but nothing has come in yet."

"So, what is this promotion?"

"I'd be based out of a different location. I'd have a direct schedule. Right now, I fly wherever and whenever the airline needs me. It would make having a life a little easier."

"So where would you be moving to?"

I cleared my throat. I wasn't sure how she would react to knowing I would move back to Seattle.

"Is it some enormous secret?" She laughed.

"I'd be moving back to Seattle."

The look that settled on her face was one I wasn't sure I wanted to see. She picked up her napkin, wiped her mouth, and took a sip of her drink. "We probably should get the bill," Harper said, glancing down at the clock on her phone. "It's getting close to boarding time."

"You're good for a bit yet," I said, glancing at my watch and signaling our server for our bill.

"I'm sorry. I just hate being late. I also hate being the last person to board the plane." She let out a tiny laugh and tried to reach for the bill that the server had placed on the table, but I grabbed it first.

"I've got it," I said, pulling it towards me and placing my credit card down on the table as and uncomfortable silence fell between us. "Are you not going to say anything?"

She looked down at the ground and shook her head. "Declan, I can't, please."

Once the bill had been paid, I walked Harper to her gate. I stood off to the side as she checked in with one of the boarding agents. She smiled as she slowly walked back over to me. "Thank you for walking me here. They are going to board in five minutes."

"Well, I should probably go then," I said, glancing at my watch.

"Yes, I guess. I wouldn't want you to be late and miss your flight."

I shrugged. "I shouldn't be. Still have lots of time."

"Despite what you may think, it was good to see you again."

"Wait, what? You mean you actually enjoyed seeing me again?"

Harper smiled and bit her bottom lip as she met my eyes and nodded.

"Would it be too much to ask you to stay in touch with me?" I questioned, pulling my card from my pocket and holding it out for her to take.

She reached out and gripped the card from my hand, her fingers brushing against mine, sending that familiar shock through me. She looked down at the card and then up to my eyes. "I think I could do that."

The airline made her boarding announcement,

and I leaned in and pulled her tightly against me, wishing that I didn't have to let her go. I felt her arms go around my neck and I closed my eyes, leaned in, and kissed the side of her neck. I whispered, "Don't make me wait too long."

CHAPTER 9

HARPER

My mind had been littered with thoughts of Declan the entire flight home. I replayed over and over everything that had happened the entire weekend, right up to the last kiss we shared and the words he had whispered in my ear before I boarded the plane.

Once I landed, I stopped at the grocery store and picked up a few things before heading back to my apartment. I showered, cooked dinner, threw in a load of laundry, and cleaned my already clean apartment to keep myself from texting Declan.

Kenzie was on her honeymoon, so I couldn't call her. I had left my work laptop at work, so I couldn't even check emails. Instead, I made my way to my bedroom, pulled the curtains, flipped the TV on, and crawled into bed. Soon I lay there staring at the ceiling, wondering what Declan was doing at this hour.

Had they delayed his plane? Was he stuck in traffic? Had he really meant what he said when he suggested that we stay in touch?

I rolled over and pulled his card off my night table and ran my fingers over the raised printing on the card. I stared at his name printed in black, fighting within myself not to text him. I knew that texting him already would make me appear desperate, so I put the card down and rolled back over onto my back, propping up my pillow.

I flipped through the channels, finding a movie, and had just gotten into it when my phone vibrated on the nightstand. I reached for it, wondering who was messaging me this late. It surprised me to see Kenzie's name on my phone.

I opened the message, fearing that something may be wrong, only to be bombarded with a slew of questions as my phone vibrated in my hand.

Kenzie: Have you forgiven Declan yet?

Kenzie: Are you guys getting back together?

Kenzie: Have you spoken to him since you have gotten home?

Kenzie: Seriously, could you answer me already?

Kenzie: I need to know or else I will not enjoy myself one bit.

Kenzie: I need to know if we are going to celebrate by being pregnant together in nine months?

I giggled to myself, the last message throwing me into a fit of laughter. I quickly replied telling her not to worry about me, to stop thinking about it and to enjoy the evening with Devon.

I waited for the next slew of text messages but the only response I received was a message telling me to go and message him, which concluded with a tongue sticking out emoji. I smiled to myself and shut the screen off and went to throw the phone back down on the nightstand when it once again vibrated with another message.

Expecting it to be Kenzie, I turned the screen back on and was shocked to see a message from Declan. Instantly, I felt warm, and my hands shook as I opened the message.

Declan: I hope you got home safely.

I felt myself smile and replied, instantly deleting what I had written.

Declan: Sweet dreams Harper.

I felt as if I were fifteen again as I lay there trying to figure out what to respond. After twenty minutes, I kept it simple and typed "you too" and hit send.

CHAPTER 10
DECLAN

I stood outside of my boss's office, excitement running through me. I'd gotten the transfer and the permanent flight schedule. I sure would miss the bustling streets of New York City, but to return to my friends and the place I grew up was exciting. My phone vibrated in my hand, and I looked down at the screen and smiled.

HARPER: Do you think you will make it for Devon and Kenzie's New Year's Eve Party?

Declan: Does that mean you want to see me again?

HARPER: Don't get your hopes up, Brookes, just thought it would be nice if you could make it.

I smiled to myself at her response. We'd spent most nights this past week texting and whenever the question came about, and I probed her for an answer on whether she wanted to see me again, the response was the same. I could imagine her sitting there smiling as she typed out her response, knowing that she was driving me crazy. I pocketed my phone as my boss stepped out of his office.

"I've had your flights covered for the next three weeks to get you moved out there. The moving company will head to your place to pack you up. Let me know if you have trouble finding a place and we will put you up for a couple of weeks in a hotel until you find an apartment."

"Great, thanks, Gary."

"No problem, Declan. Let me know if you need anything."

"Will do," I said.

Twenty minutes later, I was headed towards my favorite coffee shop. I was excited as I allowed the thoughts of being able to return home to my friends and hopefully to Harper. Things seemed to go well between us. Communication had opened and from texting we had even squeezed in a few phone calls that ended up lasting well past midnight. Last night had been the latest, I could almost hear her sleepy voice now as she had struggled not to fall asleep on me.

I had just sat down in my usual booth in the front window of the Java King when my phone rang.

"Hey, Devon. How was the honeymoon?" I answered.

"Hey, man, it was great. Listen, Kenzie and I want to know if you are going to make it to our New Year's Eve party this year?"

I chuckled, "Man, Harper has been asking me as well."

"Does that mean you two are back together?"

"No, just talking, but at least it's a start."

"That's great, man. I am so happy to hear that."

"Same. So here is the thing. I haven't given her a definite answer yet."

"Not sure you can make it? Flight schedule going crazy because of the holidays?"

"No, it's not that. I just found out I am moving back to Seattle. I haven't told her about that either. I was thinking I would keep them both a secret and surprise her at your party. Think you guys can help me out?"

"I can, but I won't let on to Kenzie. Those two are inseparable and she'd probably spill the beans."

I laughed into the phone. "All right, man, sounds good. I'll be there."

"Great, we will see you then. If you need a place to stay, you got one."

"Thanks, Devon. I appreciate it."

I hung up and took a sip of my hot coffee and turned my attention back to my messages with Harper. I read her words carefully and dialed her number.

"Hello."

"Hey."

"Declan? What are you doing calling me in the middle of a workday?"

"It's easier than typing. I know how badly you wanted to see me; however, I just got my flight schedule for the week between Christmas and New Year's. I am sad to say that I won't be able to make it to their party."

The phone was silent, and I smiled to myself. This would be worth it to see the surprise on her face when I showed up to the party.

"Oh. Um, okay, well, that's too bad. You're going to miss out."

"You know, you are horrible at hiding how you really feel there. I know you want to see me."

"Get over yourself, Brookes. It would have been nice to have you there this year after the wedding is all. I know that Devon and Kenzie both would have loved to have the four of us together again. Listen, I have to go. I have a meeting to get to."

I could hear the lump in her throat and could feel the excitement building at the fact that she really wanted to see me again.

"Okay, talk soon?"

"Yep."

CHAPTER 11

HARPER

I hung up the phone and looked around my office. My eyes burned. Why was I getting so upset at the fact that Declan couldn't make it to this party? This was ridiculous. We shared a few calls; we'd talked about our lives and it felt as if we'd barely been apart. Perhaps one or two conversations had become heated, and I had wished that he had been there in the bedroom. However, being so upset I could cry was only plain silly. I wiped my eyes and cleared the enormous lump that sat in my throat and glanced at the clock. I had to meet Kenzie for lunch.

I grabbed my coat off the hook on the door, flung my purse over my shoulder and raced out of the office and down the elevator. I was late, as usual, thanks to that phone call, so it was a good thing that we were meeting at our usual place, just around the corner from my office. I was looking forward to a steaming bowl of French onion soup for lunch.

I was just about to the door of the restaurant when I heard my name and turned to see Kenzie waving at me from across the street.

"Hey!" I shouted, waving in excitement. I watched as she ran across the busy street. "How was the honeymoon?" I asked, wrapping my arms around her.

"Amazing. Everything was perfect."

"I'm glad to hear that. I'm starving," I said, pulling the door to the restaurant open.

Kenzie ducked into the washroom while I sat in the same booth we always had and pulled my phone from my purse. There were three more messages from Declan after our call and I smiled to myself as I read each one and quickly typed out a response, shoving my phone back in my purse just as Kenzie appeared. I did my best to wipe the look from my face.

She sat down across from me and took one look at me. "Why do you look as if you are hiding something?" she questioned.

"What do you mean?" I asked.

"The smile, the blushing, what is going on?"

"Nothing. I'm winded is all."

"Oh no, no way. You aren't getting off that easy, besides you work out every day. So tell me, what's going on?"

Just as she said that my phone pinged with a message and I glanced down at my purse and smiled, knowing full well that Declan had responded to what I had said.

"You guys ready for the New Year's Eve party?" I asked, doing my best to change the subject.

"All right, fine. If you don't want to tell me, it's up to you. The answer to your question is yes, everything is almost all decorated and ready for the Christmas and the New Year's Eve party. We just need to work on what we are serving. You are still planning on coming, right, and helping me with everything?"

"Of course. I wouldn't miss it." My cell phone went off again, and I glanced once again at my purse, this time pulling out my phone and reading the message.

"Look at you."

"Look at me what?" I asked, looking up and meeting Kenzie's eyes.

"You guys are finally talking again?"

I looked at my best friend. I couldn't hold back my excitement any longer. I nodded and smiled. "Yes."

"It's about damn time. You finally forgave him?"

I searched myself for a few moments, thinking over everything that had happened at the wedding and over the past few weeks. "I guess you could say I have."

"I'm so happy to hear that. You look happy."

"I am happy. I just wish that he were closer, so we could give our relationship another try."

"Well, did you invite him to the party? Perhaps that could start things."

"I did, but he can't go. He said his flight schedule is crazy that weekend. Besides, it would only be for that weekend." I looked down at the phone, wishing that he could be there.

"What is it?"

"I just don't think it would work, us being that far away from one another. Then add on his work sched-ule, plus mine."

"You will never know if you don't try."

I shrugged. Kenzie was right, but I also wasn't sure I could enter a long-distance relationship with him. It would take me a long time to trust again.

"You know I am right," Kenzie said, reaching across the table and placing her hand on mine.

"I do. However, there is no sense in even thinking any more about it."

I looked at Kenzie and did my best to smile. "All right, so what are you wanting to serve at this party?" I asked, changing the subject, because the thought of Declan not being able to be here with me was suddenly killing me inside.

I sat in front of the TV, wrapping jalapeno poppers in phyllo dough when my phone rang. I wiped my hands on a towel and answered, tucking the phone between my shoulder and chin. "Hello."

"Hey, how are you doing?"

"Hey, I thought you were flying tonight?"

"No, they canceled my flight."

"Oh, well that sucks, I bet watching fireworks from the sky would be amazing."

"To be honest, we don't really have time to do that." Declan chuckled into the phone.

"So, now that they have cancelled your flight, and you aren't coming to the New Year's Eve party, what are your plans?"

"I'd hoped to ring in the New Year on the phone with you."

Immediately I felt my heart rate increase and then

the realization that I'd be with Kenzie and Devon until after midnight sunk in.

"Well, that would be great, but I'll be at the party."

"Can't you sneak away? Say at eleven?

"I can try. Did you want me to call you when I get back here?"

Declan didn't answer, and I stopped rolling jalapeno poppers and waited for him to say something.

"Declan, are you there?"

"I'm here. I'd love nothing more than to have you call me. I'd rather be there with you instead, but I will settle for the next best thing."

My heart melted at his words and I struggled with what to say. Finally, I just said the words that sat on the tip of my tongue, "I miss you Declan, I wish you were here."

Declan was quiet, and I felt the heat rise in my cheeks, "and on that note, I'm going to finish wrapping these jalapeno poppers."

"Have a good night. I'll talk to you soon."

"Good night Declan."

CHAPTER 12

HARPER

A thirteen-foot Christmas tree stood in the centre window of Devon and Kenzie's condo, its lights sparkling for everyone to see. Everything looked perfect, I thought to myself as I carried out a large tray of sushi and set it in the centre of the food table. Kenzie came rushing out of the kitchen with a tray of cookies and placed it over by the other desserts.

"Looks like everything is finished and ready for tonight," she said, straightening another dish on the table and resting her hands on her hips.

"Yes, I think that is everything. Oh, I left the tray of other sweets for midnight in the laundry room. There is still the tuna casserole and jalapeno poppers that I brought in the fridge too."

"Perfect! Oh, where did you put the vodka and gin I asked you to pick up?"

"I think it's still down in my car." I rushed to the door and slipped my shoes on and grabbed my keys.

"No worries. I grabbed it, Harper," Devon called from the kitchen.

"Thank you!" I yelled back.

Both Kenzie and I walked into the kitchen to find Devon standing there with three full glasses of the Cranberry Gin Holiday drink he had found online. He handed us each a glass. "A toast to another wonderful year," he said, holding up his drink.

We clinked our glasses together, and each took a sip, my eyes lighting up at the taste. "This is fantastic, Devon."

"Yes, babe, it's delicious," Kenzie said, leaning in for a quick kiss which turned into a show that I almost had to avert my eyes from.

"Why don't you two get a room." I giggled.

They quickly parted, Devon turning to finish filling the cups with more punch, when the doorbell rang.

"Eeek, they are already arriving," Kenzie said excitedly, and both of us ran to the door to welcome the guests.

I spent the night mingling with guests, making sure the food was always full, along with making more punch and helping Devon with the drinks. I did everything I could to take my mind off the fact that Declan was not here. It was almost eleven thirty, as I glanced around at all the couples in the room. It was going to be another lonely New Year's Eve, I thought to myself as I gathered some used cups to take into the kitchen.

"Hey, I think I am going to head out," I whispered to Kenzie as I dumped another handful of cups into the garbage.

"What? Already? Why?"

"What's ready?" Devon asked, coming into the kitchen with an empty tray that had held the cookies.

"Harper says she is going to head out."

"No way, you can't. You're not ringing in the new year alone."

"Devon, please," I pleaded. "It's all good. I'll be all tucked in, safe and sound, before the roads get busy."

"What fun would that be? Plus, you'd miss my New Year's kiss," he said, scooping me in his arms and twirling me around the kitchen causing me to laugh.

Kenzie smiled at me. "See, you have to stay."

"Really, guys, please. I'm going to go."

"Actually, I need your help with something," Devon bit out. "I'll be back." I watched as he took off, disappearing out of sight, wondering what he could need my help with that Kenzie couldn't do.

"See, now you have to wait. Come on, let's go back out and get things ready for the countdown," Kenzie said, grabbing my arm along with the bag of party favors we had purchased for the end of the night.

We had handed out all the favors and now stood in front of the TV, the last twenty seconds before we were to ring in the new year. Everyone stood with their significant others, arms wrapped around each other, as everyone counted down. I was hardly in the mood to be here, and I didn't want Declan to think I had stood him up, because I hadn't. I put on a brave face and counted down with the rest of them, and then would sneak out and call Declan right away.

"Three, two, one.... Happy—"

Startled at the feel of hands on my hips, I spun as everyone kissed. I was surprised to see Declan standing behind me as he finished whispering the words, "Happy New Year."

I slowly turned around, and he pulled me against him, bending to meet my lips. I could feel the tears building as I wrapped my arms around him, losing myself in his kiss, still shocked that he was standing here.

"Are you surprised?" he asked once we had parted.

I didn't know what to say, and I knew I couldn't hide the reaction on my face. I looked to my best friend, who stood there with the biggest smile.

"I told you you couldn't go home," Kenzie said, resting her head on Devon's shoulder as she smiled at the pair of us.

I looked back at Declan, still having a hard time believing he was standing in front of me.

"So, are you happy to see me?" he asked, resting his hand on the side of my cheek.

"Brookes..."

"You are a horrible liar." He smiled as he leaned in and kissed me again, silencing me from giving him my usual answer, this time his tongue sweeping through my mouth and making me weak in the knees. I didn't know what to say when we parted. I just looked up into his blue eyes, thankful that I had somehow found it in my heart to forgive him.

"What do you say, will this be our year?" he whispered, kissing the side of my neck.

"I sure hope so..." I whispered back and met his lips for another kiss, the sounds of "Auld Lang Syne" playing in the background.

Other books releasing in the Christmas of Love collection are as follows and can be read as complete standalone stories in any order.

13 Nights of Christmas by Emily Rose
Coal For Kiera by E.M. Shue
Fabricated Christmas by Glenna Maynard
Finding Mistletoe by AJ Alexander
Finding Mrs. Claus by Leaona Luxx
Holiday Wishes by S.L. Sterling
Holly's Knight by KL Donn
Merry & Bright by Mayra Statham
Secretly Sant by B.L. Olson
The Christmas Proposition by Mika Jolie
Wedding Bell Rock by Annelise Reynolds & Dawn Sullivan

Find all information about each book on the Alluring
Write Productions website.

FIRESIDE LOVE

Coming November 6, 2020

Kristy I hated my job. I had no social life. Somehow I had become so predictable after my last relationship ended, that the cashier at the local food mart already had my favorite wine bagged and waiting for me behind the counter when I walked in on Friday afternoon. I needed to get away, from everything. So when my best friend, Addie, called up and offered me a **FREE** weekend getaway, how could I say no. Promises of a quiet weekend with a good book, warm fires, and flannel pajamas? Yes, please! Austin It had been eighteen months. Eighteen months, since I had lost my wife in a car accident and learned that our marriage had been nothing but one big lie. I'd done nothing but work and mope around my sister's house, so when she told me to take her cabin for the weekend. Time alone, surrounded by nature and the fresh cold mountain air was exactly what I'd been needing. However, my plans of being alone in the wilderness quickly vanished when I walked through the doors of the cabin and found my sister's best friend drunk and half-naked on the floor of the very same cabin. I'd hidden my crush on her for years. Perhaps, not well enough. After all, Addie must have set this up. The weekend was about to get a lot more interesting. From USA Today Bestselling Author S.L. Sterling comes this friends to lovers romance that will warm your heart on a cold winters night

Read the first chapter of Fireside Love
www.authorslsterling.com/firesidelove

Get Fireside Love today.

Dear Readers,

I would like to thank you for taking the time to read *Holiday Wishes*. I hope you enjoyed Declan and Harper's story. If you did, I would love it if you would drop me a review. Reviews are so important and really help me; plus I love to hear what my readers think.

I find it hard to believe that this dreaded year is almost finally over, and I look forward to bringing you more stories of the Vegas MMA Series in the New Year. Thank you all for your support! I wish you all a very Merry Christmas and a Happy New Year!

Coming in 2021

Feb: Saviour Boy (All American Boy's Series)
March/April: Ace (Book 2 Vegas MMA)
June: Constraint (KBWorlds: Everyday Heroes)

ABOUT THE AUTHOR

S.L. Sterling had been an avid reader since she was a child, often found getting lost in books. Today, if she isn't writing or plotting, she can be found buried in a romance novel. S.L. Sterling lives with her husband and dogs in Northern Ontario.

Facebook: https://www.facebook.com/hearomance
Follow me on Bookbub http://
bit.ly/SLSterlingBookbub
Instagram http://bit.ly/SLSterlingInstagram
Goodreads http://bit.ly/SLSterlingGoodreads
Pinterest http://bit.ly/SLSterlingPinterest
Twitter http://bit.ly/SLSterlingTwitter
Newsletter: http://bit.ly/GetmyNewsletter
Website: https://www.authorslsterling.com

Join my Street Team
Sterlings Silver Sapphires: http://
bit.ly/SterlingsSapphires